Julia Wu

Laura Wu

MOUSE'S FIRST CHRISTMAS

Lauren Thompson

ILLUSTRATED BY

Buket Erdogan

SIMON & SCHUSTER BOOKS FOR YOUNG READERS

To Kevin   L.T.

To Mom, Dad, and my husband, Yucel   B.E.

SIMON & SCHUSTER
BOOKS FOR YOUNG READERS
An imprint of Simon & Schuster Children's Publishing Division

Text copyright © 1999 by Lauren Thompson
Illustrations copyright © 1999 by Buket Erdogan
All rights reserved.
SIMON & SCHUSTER BOOKS FOR YOUNG READERS
is a trademark of Simon & Schuster.
Book design by Heather Wood
Printed in Hong Kong
ISBN 0-689-82325-8 / LC 98-24073
10 9 8 7 6 5 4 3 2 1

first
edition

'Twas a night still and starry
and all through the house,
not a creature was stirring...

just one little mouse.

Mouse was peeking all around
to see what good things
could be found.

Up on the table,
Mouse found something
sweet and sparkly...

It was a
cookie.

and something
warm and melty...

It was hot cocoa.

and something
cool and sticky.

It was a candy cane.

Next to the window,
Mouse found something
jingly and glinty...

It was a jingle bell.

and something
bright and flickery...

It
was
a
candle.

and something
fine and silvery.

It was an angel.

High on the mantle,
Mouse found something
soft and felty...

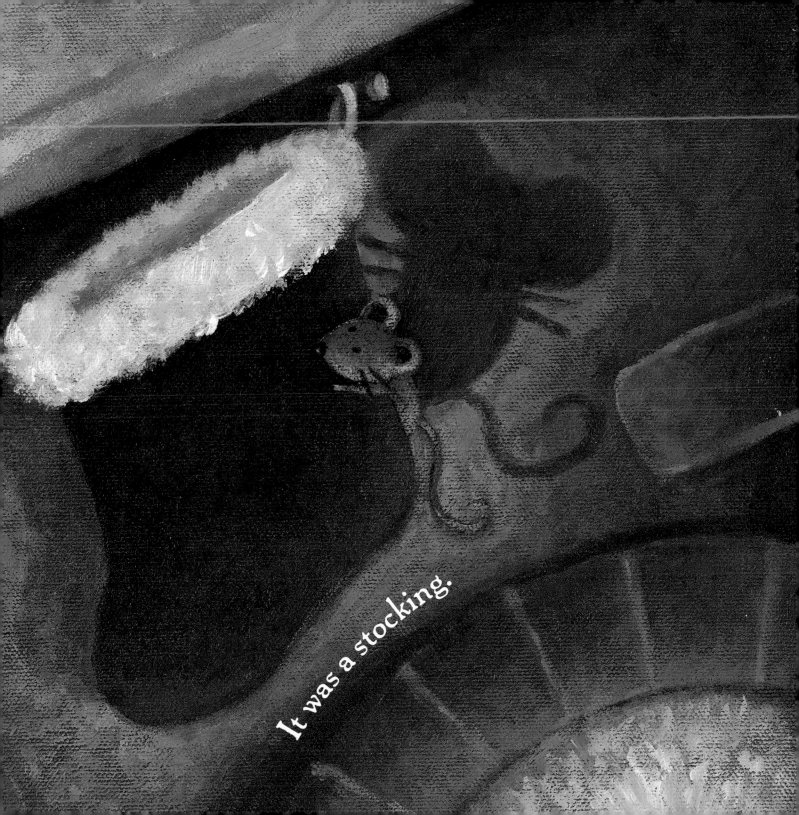

It was a stocking.

and something
white and floaty...

It
was
a
snow
globe.

and something
tinkly and twirly.

It was a music box.

Then there in the corner,
Mouse found something
tall and prickly...

It
was
a
tree.

and something
boxy and ribbony—
lots and lots of them!

Presents!

Then Mouse
found someone
whiskery
and jolly.

It was Santa Claus!

And Santa whispered,
"'Tis your very first Christmas
and all through the house
no one is loved more
than you,...

little mouse."